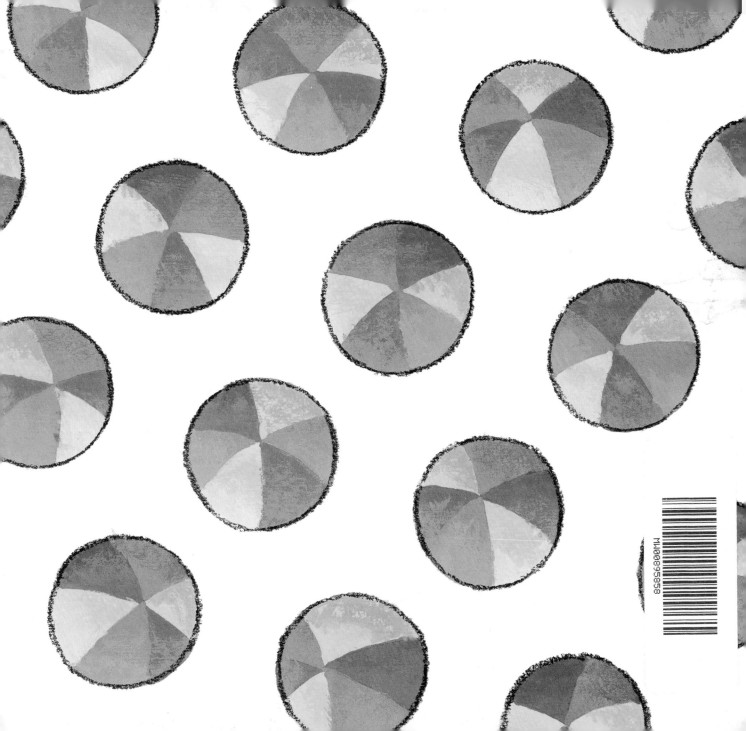

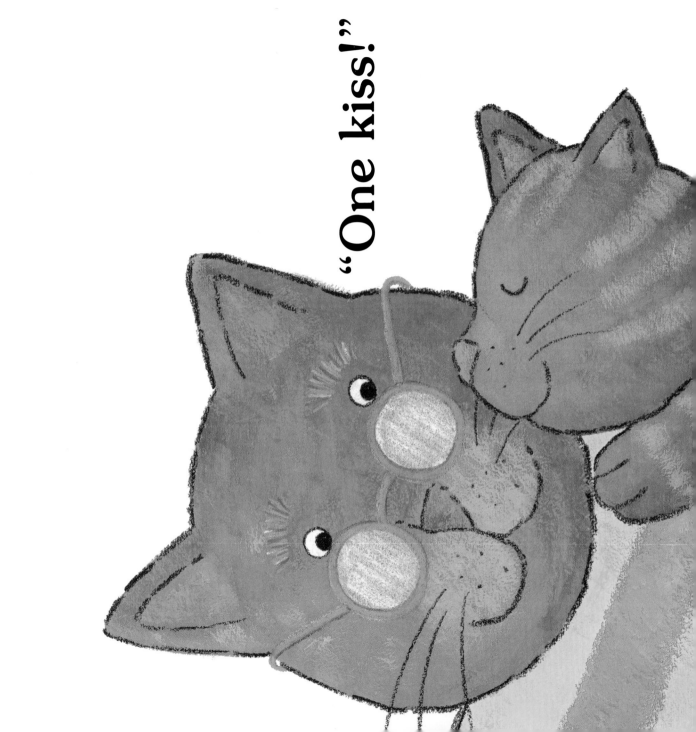

"No more books today," said Grandpa.
"I have to meet Grandma at the store."

"Now do you have a kiss for Grandpa?"
asked Louie's mother.

Grandpa read two books.

"Two more," said Louie.
"Please . . ."

"Let's read," said Grandpa.

"Okay," said Louie.

"No more cake," said Louie.
"I want to go home."

"This is good plum cake," said Grandpa.

"It's not plum," said Louie. "It's blueberry."

"Well, I like it anyway," said Grandpa.

Louie added water and beach plums, then gave Grandpa some cake to taste.

"Do you need seaweed for flavor?" asked Grandpa.

"No seaweed," said Louie.

"Now what?" asked Grandpa.

"Let's make a cake," answered Louie.

"No sand castle!"
said Louie.

"Don't run me over!"
said Grandpa.

"Should we build a sand castle?"
Grandpa asked.

"Let's play marching band," said Louie.
"I'm the leader. You follow me."

Grandpa tooted. Louie banged.

Rum-a-tee,
Rum-a-tee,
Rum-a-tee, TUM!

"No ball!"

"Do you want to play ball?"
Grandpa asked.

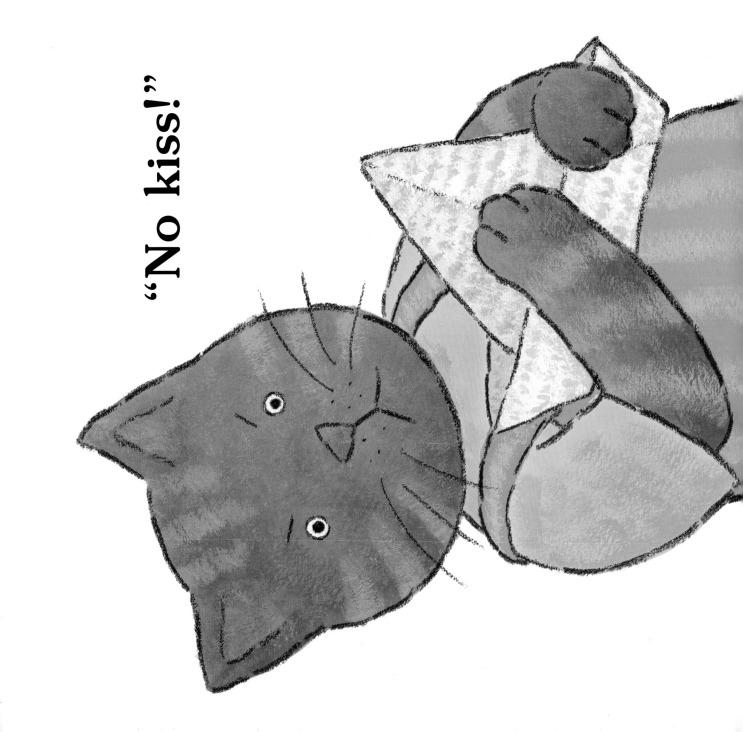

"No kiss!"

"Do you have a kiss for Grandpa?"
Louie's mother asked.

Louie was busy. His mother said,
"Shoes and socks on. Grandpa is
waiting for you."

For my grandfather, Isaac Godlin

—H.Z.

To Oma Krul, the best grandmother I could
ever wish for

—E.B.

Orchard Books
An Imprint of Scholastic Inc.
95 Madison Avenue
New York, NY 10016

Printed in China for Harriet Ziefert, Inc.
The text of this book is set in 18 point Souvenir Medium.
The illustrations are gouache.

10 9 8 7 6 5 4 3 2 1

Library of Congress Cataloging-in-Publication Data
Ziefert, Harriet.
No kiss for Grandpa / by Harriet Ziefert ; illustrated by Emilie Boon.
p.   cm.
Summary: After he and his grandfather spend the day doing what Louie wants to do, the young kitten gives Grandpa the best kiss ever.
ISBN 0-531-30328-4 (alk. paper)
[1. Cats—Fiction. 2. Grandfathers—Fiction.] I. Boon, Emilie, ill. II. Title.
PZ7.Z487   Nk   2001   [E]—dc21   00-44095

No Kiss for Grandpa

Harriet Ziefert

pictures by Emilie Boon

Orchard Books / New York

An Imprint of Scholastic Inc.